The Little Scrub Christmas Tree

To: Anne & Lillian
From: Scrubby
   I hope that you enjoy reading
about scrubby's experience and also
learn a new lesson. I wish you
both all the best
    Dr. Raymond Dunn

Dr. Raymond Dunn

ISBN-13: 9781974365296
ISBN-10: 1974365298

This book is dedicated to Darrien, Amara, and to all of my grand-children for the character roles they played in this story or the inspiration I drew from them in writing this book.

With love,
Granddad

DARRIEN

AMARA

HUNTER

DANIEL

KING

JADEN

KELSO

KAI

CHRISTIAN

KELS

KYLAHNI

ZELAYA

COBE

DYLAN

DESTINEE-RAE

ZAHAYLI

ZACHARI

KALIL

The Little Scrub Christmas Tree

O nce there was a robin bird who told a story about a beautiful Christmas-tree farm that was located on many acres of rolling hills. When the wind blew, the trees swayed from left to right and made enchanting music as the air flowed swiftly through their limbs, and when the wind stopped blowing, they stretched their limbs to the sky to soak up the warm rays of the sun.

He told how the farmer planted new Christmas-tree seedlings each spring to replace the trees harvested during the last Christmas season. The farmer tried to grow the biggest and prettiest trees, because the biggest and best trees would be selected next Christmas to be placed in special locations around the world for millions and millions of people to see.

Many different types of Christmas trees grew on the farm: There was Roots, a tall Colorado blue spruce; Bark, a big strong Fraser fir; Cone, a Norway spruce who kept to himself; and Needles, a noble fir who loved to be in charge. Jaden, a white fir, and his little cousin Baby Bump, a Douglas fir, just admired their big siblings and stayed out of the way.

The trees were beautiful, and they tried to outdo one another. Roots loved showing off his long, thin pine needles. Bark took pride in his beautiful shape. Cone claimed to have the prettiest pinecones and the most triangular form. Needles said he was the best because his pine needles were soft and stayed fresh for a long, long time.

The farmer loved the competition between the trees because it inspired each of them to look its best. Each soaked up as much sun as it could and lapped up as many minerals as possible so that it could grow taller and prettier than the other trees.

Down the road from the Christmas-tree farm was a vast forest of scrub pines. Scrub pines grow wild in the forest without the special care of a tree farmer. No one grooms, fertilizes, or waters scrub pines; they are left to grow on their own and maybe one day become firewood. A long fence made of wood and wire separated the beautiful Christmas-tree farm from the ugly scrub-pine forest. But the fence, with all its wire, could not stop birds from flying from one forest to the other.

One day, robin bird and a large blue-and-black crow named King perched themselves high on a tall scrub pine—the tallest and strongest scrub pine in the scrub forest. When they flew away, they passed right over the Christmas-tree farm. Little did King know that stuck to his foot was a tiny pine seed. As fate would have it, the wind blew the seed off King's foot, and it fell into the dirt in the middle of the Christmas-tree farm. The robin bird told King about the seed, and they wondered what would happen, because only Christmas trees grew on the farm. Thereafter, every time they flew over the farm, they looked anxiously at the spot where the seed had fallen.

After many weeks of rain and sunshine, a little green stem pushed its way up through the dirt. The little pine stem pushed and pushed until it had three little limbs above the ground. The stubby limbs swayed in the wind as the little scrub pine tried to anchor its roots deep into the soil.

When the Christmas trees saw the little scrub pine, there was much chatter throughout the farm. Roots, the Colorado blue spruce, asked, "What is this thing growing among us?"

Sap, a white fir, asked, "Where did it come from?"

Bark, the Fraser fir, replied, "Don't worry about him. He isn't a Christmas tree. He could never be important and beautiful like us."

Christian, a beautiful balsam fir, said, "Let's ask King, the crow, what type of tree it is. He has seen many forests."

So they asked King, who said with pride in his voice, "It's a scrub pine from the forest down the road. When it grows up, I can sit on its treetop and see for miles and miles around."

"Well, you won't sit atop that one," said Needles, the noble fir, "because when the farmer sees it, surely he will chop it down."

"That's right," said Roots. "Nothing grows here but true Christmas trees like us."

Hastily, King replied, "But in the forest, we have many different types of trees, and they all serve a special purpose. We have oak trees that grow large and stately and birch trees with pretty leaves and white bark. The redwoods are huge—even I have trouble flying to their tops. And don't forget the walnut trees that provide homes for birds and squirrels and wood for humans to make into furniture. The maple trees give sap so sweet that humans make syrup from it."

"Those things are not as important as we are," said Cone. "People take us into their homes at Christmastime and decorate us with ornaments, lights, snowflakes, and garlands. They play music and lay gifts under us, and at our very top, they place a glowing angel or star. Surely we are the most important trees of all."

To which King replied, "Ornaments, lights, and celebrations last only for a season." And away he flew.

The little scrub pine had listened carefully to the conversation happening high overhead. After hearing what the Christmas trees said, he did not feel very important. As a matter of fact, his limbs began to sag, and his pine needles no longer pointed upward to the sky. For days and days, the little scrub pine drooped and drooped, until one morning, a ladybug named Kels lit on his pine needle. Kels liked the little scrub pine and decided to name him Scrubby. He was short and scraggly and different and just the right size for her to make her home on his branches. That made Scrubby feel important, and Scrubby and Kels soon became the best of friends.

One day while Kels was flying around the Christmas-tree farm, she saw a large red tractor pulling a plow that was coming in Scrubby's direction. Also, there were several men with sharp tools chopping down the weeds that were growing between the rows of trees and with sharp shears that they used to trim the branches of the Christmas trees. Kels hurriedly flew back to warn Scrubby of what was coming. She was sure that either the tractor or the men would cut Scrubby down.

The Christmas trees saw the tractor and men coming and became very excited. For them, the workers' attentions were like getting their hair cut or their nails polished. A trim from the workers was almost as good as getting fitted for a brand-new suit or a lovely new dress. Suddenly, throughout the Christmas-tree farm, the trees were arguing over who would look the best after the workers trimmed and shaped them and cleared the weeds from around their trunks.

Throughout the farm, the argument waged on as to who would be selected and, more importantly, which type of tree had been selected the oftenest. Young trees like Jaden and Baby Bump had nothing to say, for it would be many years before their day. They had not yet withstood the test of time, the scorching summers with no rain to be found, nor the long, cold winters with snow weighing their branches down.

The competition was serious. The trees knew that the tallest and shapeliest among them would be selected at Christmas time to be sent to very special places like the White House, where the president lived, Rockefeller Center in New York City, Trafalgar Square in London, the Reichstag building in Berlin, or Rio de Janeiro to become the Lagoa floating Christmas tree, as well as town centers all over the world. Only the tallest and most perfectly formed trees would be selected for those locations. The trees selected would be seen by millions and millions of people. They would be decorated with hundreds and thousands of decorations of all kinds. The special trees would be seen on televisions across the land, and hundreds and thousands of people would stand in line to speak to Santa, seated under them. Oh, what a wonderful honor it would be to carry on the family tradition of being selected as a special tree!

Scrubby asked the big trees around him, "Who was selected for those special honors last year?"

Proudly, Needles replied, "My dad was selected for the White House, and the year before, my uncle was sent to the Rockefeller Center."

"Oh my," said Scrubby. "You come from a very important family."

Roots, who'd almost been selected himself, replied, "My grandfather was chosen last year for Trafalgar Square."

Bark proudly stated, "Three of my family members have been selected."

Christian smiled at Scrubby and answered, "My mother was the first lady to be selected as a special tree."

"That is wonderful," said Scrubby. "I wonder if my mom, dad, or grandparents were ever selected for a special honor." The other trees did not respond. Scrubby felt a little embarrassed. "Well, I guess not. People don't look for the best and prettiest where I come from."

Scrubby warily eyed the slowly approaching workers, with Kels nestling nervously in his branches with her eyes closed. He searched his mind for a reason the workers might let him grow; he knew being a home for a ladybug probably wasn't enough. He wished he could ask his mom or dad what to do; you can always depend on your parents when you need good advice, but he had no one. His friends the robin bird, King, and the wise old owl could do nothing but cover their eyes with their wings and tell Scrubby to be brave.

As the workers drew nearer to Scrubby, there came into view a young boy who had come to work with his father to see how the men cared for the Christmas trees. The farmer only allowed experienced workers to attend to his expensive trees, so it was very unusual to see a young boy with the men, but this boy, whose name was Hunter, was the farmer's son, and he wanted to learn all about the beautiful trees. Hunter wasn't allowed to hoe, trim, or shape the trees yet—he could only watch and pass tools to the grown-ups.

When the workers finally reached the spot where Scrubby was growing, they saw that he was not a Christmas-tree and angrily called for the tractor to push him over and haul him away. Kels began to cry, King started cawing, and the robin bird pecked at the tractor. The commotion caught Hunter's attention, and he rushed over to see what the excitement was all about. Hunter noticed how different the little tree was. It was not as tall or as full or as strong as the other trees of its age. But there was something about the little tree that caught the boy's attention, like a promise that could not yet be seen.

As the tractor pulled up to Scrubby and prepared to push him over, Cone, Sap, Bark, and Roots watched with high expectation of seeing the end of Scrubby, but Christian wasn't so sure. She noticed the admiring look in Hunter's eyes and the pounding of his heart as he walked around Scrubby, stroking each branch tenderly with his hand. When his father walked up, Hunter begged him to let him hoe, trim, and care for this little tree, since it was not an expensive Christmas tree like the others. His father reluctantly agreed and stopped the tractor. Hunter did his best to fertilize, clear the weeds, shape, and trim Scrubby. Thereafter, every year at tree-trimming time, Hunter would go with his father and the other men to care for the Christmas trees, but he only cared for Scrubby, the little scrub pine that he adopted as his own.

Several years passed as Hunter and Scrubby grew up together, and as Hunter's arms and legs grew longer, Scrub's limbs grew longer, and his trunk stretched taller. Over the years, Hunter received many compliments from his father and the workers on how beautifully he had grown and trimmed Scrubby. As a matter of fact, over the years, several farm workers asked to buy Scrubby for their own home because he was so beautiful, but with every request, Hunter said, "Thank you for the offer, but this tree is special and is not for sale."

Scrub's growth did not go unnoticed by the big Christmas trees. There was much talk as he grew taller and stronger and his shape filled out and his once-rough needles became softer and rounder. The first time Hunter trimmed Scrubby, all the trees laughed and asked, "Why is he trimming that scraggly runt? And what is a little boy doing on our Christmas-tree farm?" They were surprised to see him return year after year and felt jealous because he only cared for Scrubby. But Scrubby's friends, Zelaya, a colorful butterfly, and Zahayli and Zachari, two honeybees, didn't laugh; they welcomed the attention Scrubby received. Over the years, they also admired the changes in his needles, shape, and height. King was happier than anyone else about Scrubby's growth, because he was responsible for dropping him there, and he hoped that one day he could sit atop Scrubby and flap his wings in the breeze.

Scrubby wasn't as tall as some of the other full-grown trees, but he was tall enough. His limbs were not as full as the Colorado spruce, the Douglas fir, or the grand fir, but they were full enough. His needles didn't stay moist as long as the white spruce, the eastern white pine, or the Fraser fir, but they stayed moist long enough. Regardless, none of that mattered to him, because Scrubby wasn't in competition for anything—he was just enjoying being special to his friends Hunter and Kels and providing a home and shade for the animals, the insects, and the birds.

But one day, some strangers arrived, and everything changed. The Christmas season was quickly approaching, and as usual, the tree-selection chatter was the main talk throughout the farm. The trees heard the cars pull in, and they watched, full of anticipation, as the strangers approached. With them was a special guest named Dylan. The trees and the animals listened to the talk among the guests, and they learned that Dylan was from the White House. Tomorrow, he would bring the president's son, Darrien, and daughter, Amara, to the Christmas-tree farm to select the special tree for the White House, called "the Blue Room Tree."

In years past, there had been many children raised in the White House: there was Baron; Sasha and Malia; Jenna and Barbara; Chelsea; Amy; Tricia; John and Caroline; Susan and Steven; Luci; Charles; the Roosevelt children; the Grant children; and the Lincoln children, but no one on the farm could ever remember any of those children making the selection of the Blue Room Tree that would be placed in the White House.

The exciting news made the Christmas-tree farm come alive with even more chatter and challenges. Needles began to shine his needles, Bark went about polishing his trunk, and Roots stretched as high as he could so as to be the tallest tree on the farm. Scrubby and all his friends thought, *Why can't everyone just be themselves and be happy for the tree that is selected?*

In past years, the special selections had always been made by adults, so no one really knew what to expect or what would impress the president's children. The wise old owl who could always be counted on for good advice and wisdom declared that this selection would be the most important Christmas-tree selection ever because the choice would not be made based on what was important to grown-ups, like money or size or location, but by the innocent judgment of children, who would make their selection based on love. With that, all the trees grew quiet and thoughtful. Now all they could do was wait for the next day.

The next morning, the president's children, Darrien and Amara, arrived at the Christmas-tree farm early, eager to see the trees.

The farmer, his son, Hunter, and a large group of reporters, TV cameras, decorators, and groundskeepers walked with the children throughout the tree farm, stopping to explain why each tree they showed was special. They pointed out every detail, including how many times and for what locations each type of tree had been selected. They showed the grand fir and told of its impressive winning record, and then they showed the Douglas fir, which was by far the tallest tree on the farm. One man asked the children, "How would you like to have that beauty in the White House?" There were many, many more trees on the farm, but the farmer thought that none of the others could compare to the ones that had been shown.

As the hour passed noon, Darrien and Amara were tired and hungry from walking around all morning. They decided that they would have lunch, after which they would make their selection. Cone knew he would be selected, because each of his beautiful brown cones was perfectly shaped. Roots was sure he would be their choice, because the children had spent the most time looking at him. Bark's trunk was shining, and he was perfectly trimmed, so he thought surely the children would select him. Needles wasn't worried—Amara had touched his needles and told Darrien how soft they were and what a sweet pine scent he had.

In no time at all, the children's lunch—a sandwich, some fruit, and a bottle of juice—was prepared. Finding a shady spot to eat was not a problem, because the trees were so tall they blocked out most of the sunlight. The adults moved away to discuss the details of cost and transporting the tree, as well as the expense of decorating and what theme the president's wife, called the first lady, might choose for the tree decorations.

While everyone was busy, Hunter sat under Scrubby and began eating lunch and reading a book. Scrubby was behind Darrien and Amara. He had not been pointed out to them, because, of course, he was just a scrub pine and wouldn't be considered anyway.

But as the children ate, they noticed how quiet it was around the trees. Roots stood tall, but he stood alone; Cone had a nice shape and lovely cones, but so did some of the other trees; Needles had soft needles, but nothing nestled in them; and Bark had a beautiful trunk, but it was lonely and bare. Christian was beautiful, and Darrien felt a special connection to her that he could not explain. Tamara gave him a pat on the back and said, "She's young; she will have her chance next year." By the time the children finished lunch, they had lost all interest in Cone, Roots, Needles, Bark, and the other trees, and they were ready to go and look someplace else.

But behind the children, lots of things were happening. When they turned in that direction, they saw a beautiful pine tree with a large black crow sitting on its top. They saw bright ladybugs, humming bees, butterflies, and lightning bugs flitting around the tree like live decorations. It was a magical sight. There was a fox, two rabbits, three squirrels, and other animals skittering in and out of sight, and the wise old owl and the robin bird were singing from within the tree's branches. No one was left out.

Now, all the other trees noticed the attention that Scrubby drew, but they didn't worry, for they all knew that Scrubby was just a scrub pine; he would never do.

Lunchtime was over as the children approached the young man reading by this miraculous tree. He put away his book and extended his hand. The children were full of questions, and he tried to assist as best he could. Questions like, "What type of tree is this? Why do the birds sing from it, songs so sweet that they sound like Christmas hymns? Why are all the animals gathered around this tree? Is there something about it that only they can see? Why do the bees and butterflies play here, like they're friends? Why does the sunlight reflect so brightly from its limbs when all the other trees are so dim?" Then they smiled at each other, and with a nod of their heads, they dismissed all the other trees and said they wanted this one instead.

By now the adults were all gathered around, and they heard what the children had said. They found it hard to believe that with all the expensive trees around, the children had selected a scrub pine for the very first time. The decision had been made, however, and Hunter had agreed that if Scrubby was what they wanted, then Scrubby was what they would indeed have.

Now the other trees were disappointed, and their limbs began to sag. The robin bird noticed, and he admonished them as follows:

You should never, ever brag.
Accept others for who and what they are.
A self-important attitude won't get you very far.
Your family, your roots, your pedigree
don't determine the kind of tree you'll be.
Don't waste your time just looking good.
Be kind at heart—you really should.

Suddenly all the trees felt better because of the lesson they had learned. They congratulated Scrubby and said they would gladly wait their turn. Scrubby, once chopped and loaded to go away, said to the trees and his friends, "I'll see you on Christmas Day."

The End

ABOUT THE AUTHOR

• • •

*D*r. Dunn holds advanced degrees in higher education administration and an undergraduate degree in elementary education. Dr. Dunn's many years of work in education include teaching at the elementary grade level as well as teaching at the college and graduate levels. Dr. Dunn served as chairman of the board for the Community Coordinated Childcare Program in Miami-Dade County, Florida. Dr. Dunn served as dean of student services at Miami Dade Community College and Lake City Community College.

Made in the USA
Middletown, DE
07 December 2017